GADGET BOY AND KID FANTASTIC

GEORGE IVANOFF
MELISSA WEBB

NELSON
CENGAGE Learning

Australia • Brazil • Japan • Korea • Mexico • Singapore • Spain • United Kingdom • United States

NELSON
CENGAGE Learning™

Gadget Boy and Kid Fantastic

Fast Forward
Purple Level 20

Text: George Ivanoff
Illustrations: Melissa Webb
Editor: Johanna Rohan
Design: Vonda Pestana
Series design: James Lowe
Production controller: Seona Galbally
Audio recordings: Juliet Hill, Picture Start
Spoken by: Matthew King and Abbe Holmes
Reprint: Jennifer Foo

ISBN 978 0 17 012660 1
ISBN 978 0 17 012657 1 (set)

Cengage Learning Australia
Level 7, 80 Dorcas Street
South Melbourne, Victoria Australia 3205
Phone: 1300 790 853

Cengage Learning New Zealand
Unit 4B Rosedale Office Park
331 Rosedale Road, Albany, North Shore NZ 0632
Phone: 0508 635 766

For learning solutions, visit cengage.com.au

Printed in Australia by Ligare Pty Ltd
7 8 9 10 11 12 13 21 20 19 18 17

POSTERA CRESCAM LAUDE
THE UNIVERSITY OF MELBOURNE

Evaluated in independent research by staff from the Department of Language, Literacy and Arts Education at the University of Melbourne.

GADGET BOY AND KID FANTASTIC

GEORGE IVANOFF · MELISSA WEBB

Contents

Chapter 1

THE INTERNATIONAL SUPERHERO CONFERENCE

"Welcome to the International
Superhero Conference!"
said the woman on stage.

Gadget Boy looked around
the auditorium.
He had never seen so many
superheroes and their sidekicks
in the same room before.
He saw Electric Grandma and Wolf Boy
and Doctor Detective
and Teen-agent ...

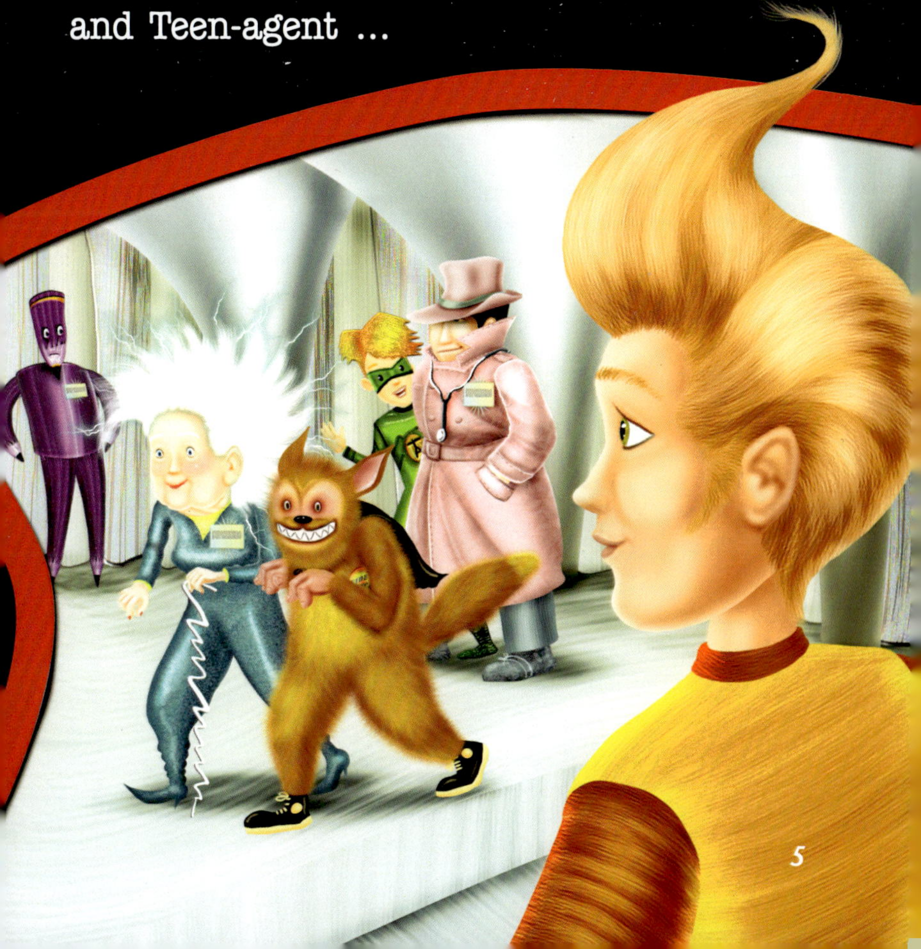

"we will share our
crime-fighting methods
and compare our superpowers."

Suddenly, there was a loud POP,
and the woman disappeared.

Gadget Boy was impressed.
"What a cool superpower!"
he said to Robo-man.
Gadget Boy was Robo-man's sidekick.

Robo-man looked worried.
"Disappearing isn't one of
Organiser Lady's superpowers,"
he said.

Gadget Boy looked worried, too.

“Where’s Organiser Lady?”
asked Hyper Woman,
as she walked through the door
of the auditorium.
“I thought the conference
had started.”
Hyper Woman was always late.

Suddenly, there was another POP
and Hyper Woman disappeared, too.

Just then, Kid Fantastic ran through
the door, shouting,
"You forgot this!"
He was holding up
a conference badge
with  on it.

His badge said  .

Chapter 2

POP! POP! POP!

POP! POP! POP!

Robo-man and Gadget Boy looked around.
More superheroes were disappearing!

"What's going on?"
asked Electric Grandma.

"I have no idea," replied Robo-man.

People jumped out of their seats as even more superheroes disappeared.

POP! POP! POP! POP!
POP! POP! POP! POP!
POP! POP! POP! POP!

"It sounds like we're in a giant popcorn maker!" laughed Kid Fantastic.

POP!

Electric Grandma disappeared.

POP!

Robo-man disappeared.

Gadget Boy and Kid Fantastic stared at each other.
All of the superheroes had disappeared – only the sidekicks were left.
Most of the sidekicks didn't know what to do without their superheroes.

"Now what?" asked Gadget Boy.

"We need to get organised," said Kid Fantastic.

Gadget Boy didn't understand what Kid Fantastic was saying.
"Shouldn't we look for the superheroes?" he asked him.

Kid Fantastic pushed past Gadget Boy
and headed for the stage.
"There are more important things
to do first!" he shouted.

"Okay, listen up, sidekicks!"
he shouted into the microphone.
The sidekicks looked up at him.
"Our superheroes have disappeared,"
he began.
"But, that's no reason to panic.
It's our turn to be in the spotlight now.
We don't need the superheroes.
There are cities out there
that need protecting!"

POP! POP! POP!

Chapter 3

THE TRACKING DEVICE

Gadget Boy knew that something
wasn't right.
He took the tracking device
from his belt.
Robo-man had a similar device
so they could always find each other.

Gadget Boy's tracking device
began to beep.
Something was very odd.
The tracking device
said that Robo-man was still
in the room.
It said he was on the stage!

Gadget Boy walked towards the stage.
The beeping grew louder and faster.
He jumped onto the stage,
using his spring-loaded boots.

"Get off the stage!"
shouted Kid Fantastic.

"I'm trying to find Robo-man,"
replied Gadget Boy.
He pointed to his tracking device.
It was beeping louder and faster.
"I don't understand.
My tracking device is saying
that Robo-man is in that box
on your belt!"

Kid Fantastic ran off the stage.
But, before he could escape,
Stretchy Girl stuck out
one of her long, stretchy legs
and tripped him up.

SAVING ALL THE SUPERHEROES

Gadget Boy jumped over
to Kid Fantastic.
He grabbed the box on
Kid Fantastic's belt.

"Don't touch the box!"
yelled Kid Fantastic.

Gadget Boy looked at the controls.
"Gadgets are my special power,"
he said, pressing the green button.

Suddenly, the room was filled
with popping sounds.
Within seconds,
all of the superheroes were back.

"What happened?" asked Robo-man.

Gadget Boy held out the box.
"Kid Fantastic used this gadget
to trap all the superheroes.
It's a computer and you were all
stored in the hard-drive."

Gadget Boy took off Robo-man's
SUPERHERO conference badge.
He turned it over and held it up
to all the superheroes.
A red light was flashing
on the back of it.
"The hard-drive trapped everyone
who was wearing a SUPERHERO
conference badge."

"But, why?" asked Hyper Woman.

"I'm sick of being a sidekick,"
shouted Kid Fantastic.
"I wanted to be a superhero,
and I wanted all the other sidekicks
to be superheroes, too."

"Some of us are happy
being sidekicks,"
smiled Gadget Boy.

"Well done, Gadget Boy!"
said Robo-man.
"It looks like you have saved
the day again!"